Joshua and Katerina
and the
Magical Broken Ornament

Joshua and Katerina
and the
Magical Broken Ornament

by
Tina Kobylinski

XULON PRESS

Xulon Press
2301 Lucien Way #415
Maitland, FL 32751
407.339.4217
www.xulonpress.com

Printed in the United States of America.

ISBN-13: 978-1-6628-0016-0
Hard Cover: 978-1-6628-0017-7
Ebook: 978-1-6628-0018-4

Introduction

My name is Tina Kobylinski, and I am so excited to see this book come to life. I am a mother and grandmother and have always had a love for children and teaching them about the love and power of God. This book began during my battle with cancer. After four years and multiple chemo treatments, I began having dreams about God's desire to heal me, which in turn became the inspiration for this children's book. I told Him that if He wanted me to remember and write this down, He would have to help me remember this the next day. After three days, I had written the storyline and then started editing it. I feel honored to have been picked by God to have written this story. I hope to write more books in the future to help children learn valuable lessons through storytelling.

There was a brother and sister whose names were Joshua and Katerina. They had just finished putting up their Christmas tree. Their parents told them they could go outside and build a snowman. A fresh winter snow had just fallen. They both looked down and saw a broken Christmas ornament laying in the snow. As they touched the ornament, they were transported to a magical kingdom.

ar off in the distance, they saw a castle. On their way toward it, they met the first of four fairies who would teach them valuable lessons. The first fairy's name was Lillianna. She was very beautiful, and she had a daughter named Piperlina. Lillianna taught them how to have faith. Faith is believing without seeing in something or someone. Joshua and Katerina said they had faith that the king of the castle was able to help them home. Because of their faith, Lillianna let them move forward.

Joshua and Katerina walked until they met the second fairy. Her name was Elizianna. She taught them about believing. Believing means to put all your confidence or faith in the truth of something or someone. Joshua and Katerina told Elizianna they wanted to learn how to truly believe the words and truth from the king and that he would help them to get home. The fairy told them that they could proceed further toward the castle.

Eventually, they met the third fairy, whose name was Levinia. She taught them about the importance of asking. Asking means requesting what you need or want. Joshua and Katerina told the fairy that they have had a good time in the crystal kingdom, however, they wanted to spend time with the king and ask him for wisdom and direction to find their way home. Levinia told them they could go forward.

Joshua and Katerina walked and walked until they finally made it to the castle. It was made of crystal and was the most beautiful place they had ever seen. There, they met the fourth fairy standing at the gate. She was a much larger fairy, and her name was Christinia. She taught them what it means to receive. To receive means to have something given to you and take it as your own. They told Christinia they wanted to meet the king. They were excited to receive all the blessings the king had to offer them. The fairy let them enter the crystal castle.

Joshua and Katerina entered the castle. They saw crystal rivers an streets of gold.

Then they saw the magnificent fairy king. As they approached, they honorably bowed to him. The king asked them what they sought of him. They told him they were excited to spend time with him and hopeful that he would help them to get home. He asked them if they had learned the four lessons from the fairies. They said they did.

The king said since they had learned all of their lessons, they may return home by touching this Christmas ornament.

As they touched the ornament, they were instantly transported back to their home. When they looked down in the snow, they saw that the broken ornament had been made whole.

Lightning Source UK Ltd.
Milton Keynes UK
UKHW052017201220
375351UK00005B/61

9 781662 800177